For Georgie
and Olivia

Tim Warnes

Happy Birthday, Dotty!

Dotty was very excited. It was her birthday, and she had lots of cards to open.

But where were all of Dotty's friends?

Dotty went to find Pip the
Mouse. Instead she found a
little round present with her
name on it!

What could it be?

Happy Birthday
Dotty!
Love from
Pip the mouse X

Hooray!

A bouncy ball!

As she chased after it for a bit,
Dotty spotted an arrow
on the floor. It pointed to
another and another.

It was a birthday trail!
Dotty followed the arrows...

to the sandbox, where there was another present. Dotty read the tag: "Happy Birthday, Dotty! Love, Tommy the Tortoise."

What was it?

Delicious!

A yummy bone!

Dotty hurried across the garden, following the arrows to...

Susie's apple tree.

Leaning against her nest was another present!

Yippee!

It was a kite from Susie!

But Susie wasn't there to help
fly it. Where was everyone?

Dotty was puzzled.
Taking all her presents,
she skipped along the trail
of arrows to . . .

Whiskers the Rabbit's hutch.

Dotty saw another funny-shaped present. She read, "Happy Birthday, Dotty! Love, Whiskers."

It was . . .

Dotty squealed with delight.
She put all her presents
into the tricycle's basket.
She'd had lots of surprises,
but Dotty's friends were
still nowhere to
be found.

Where could they be?
Maybe they had followed
the arrows too. Dotty
climbed onto her
shiny new tricycle
and . . .

Whee!

She went to look for her friends.

Suddenly the trail ended.

Dotty was amazed to find . . .

the
biggest present
she had ever seen!

Dotty danced around
and around in circles.
What could this be?

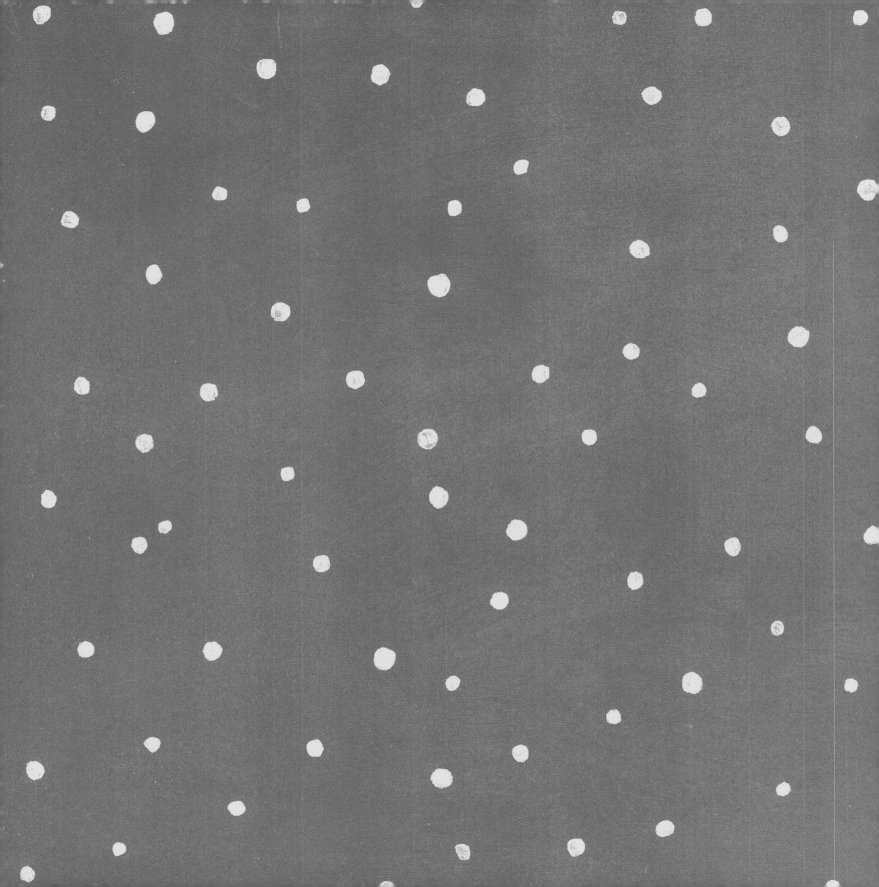